For my dear husband, Fred, and our own smoochable pooch, Barkly.
-T. S.

Text copyright © 2010 by Teddy Slater.
Illustrations copyright © 2010 by Arthur Howard.

All rights reserved. Published by Scholastic Inc.
SCHOLASTIC, CARTWHEEL BOOKS, and associated logos are trademarks and/or registered trademarks of Scholastic Inc.

Library of Congress Cataloging-in-Publication Data
Slater, Teddy.
Smooch your pooch / by Teddy Slater ; illustrated by Arthur Howard.–1st ed.   p. cm.
Summary: Illustrations and rhyming text suggest many different ways
to show your dog you love him, from taking him on a hike to throwing him a ball or a stick.
ISBN 978-0-545-16736-9 (hardcover)
[1. Stories in rhyme. 2. Dogs-Fiction.] I. Howard, Arthur, ill. II. Title.
PZ8.3.S6318Sm 2011   [E]–dc22   2010010212

ISBN 978-0-545-16736-9

10 9 8 7 6 5 4 3 2 1   10 11 12 13 14

Designed by Angela Jun
Printed in Singapore   46
First edition, October 2010

SMOOCH Your POOCH

By Teddy Slater

Illustrations by Arthur Howard

Cartwheel
B·O·O·K·S ®

SCHOLASTIC INC.

New York   Toronto   London   Auckland   Sydney   Mexico City   New Delhi   Hong Kong

Smooch your pooch to show that you care.

Give him a hug
anytime, anywhere.

Toss him a bone.
Feed him some kibble.

Or better yet, pizza.
He'd sure like a nibble.

Get out your fiddle and play a sweet song.
Musical pups will love howling along.

Tickle his belly.
Rub his soft snout.

When he woofs at the door,
    let him go right on out.

Some dogs love
to paddle.

Some dogs love to roll.

But all dogs love digging
a nice messy hole.

So, if he's your buddy,
    just let him get muddy.

There are so many wonderful
things you can do
for the four-legged friend
who's so loyal to you.

Throw him some
tennis balls:

ONE

TWO

THREE

FOUR.

You can't throw too many —
he'll always want more.

Throw him a stick.
Throw him a Frisbee.

**To make your dog happy,
    you must keep him busy.**

Take him along when you go for a hike.

Save him a seat
    when you pedal your bike.

Let him sit by your side when you go for a ride.
And make sure that the window is opened up wide.

When his ears get all flappy,
you'll know your dog's happy!

When he's all tuckered out and it's time for a nap,
give him some space on the couch

. . . or your lap.

Some dogs love
to snuggle.

Some dogs love to dance.

If yours wants to skateboard,
then give him a chance.

But most of all, love him
and give him a kiss.
He'll kiss you right back
with a smooch just like this.